THE FALLEN

THE FALLEN

Jason M. Burns

DARBY CREEK
MINNEAPOLIS

Darby Creek
An imprint of Lerner Publishing Group, Inc.
241 First Avenue North
Minneapolis, MN 55401 USA

For reading levels and more information, look up this title at www.lernerbooks.com.

Image credits: Photointoto/Shutterstock (angel wings); Rosen Graphic/Shutterstock (texture); idwan kurnia/Shutterstock (font); PERFECT_VECTORS/Shutterstock (font).

Main body text set in Janson Text LT Std.
Typeface provided by Adobe Systems.

Library of Congress Cataloging-in-Publication Data

Names: Burns, Jason M., 1978–author
Title: The fallen / Jason M. Burns.
Description: Minneapolis : Darby Creek, 2026. | Series: Demon hunter | Audience term: Teenagers | Audience: Ages 11–18 | Audience: Grades 7–9 | Summary: When a mysterious biker gang comes to town and causes chaos in Salem while also battling demons, Damon and his fellow demon hunters must uncover whether the gang is a secret ally or something far more dangerous.
Identifiers: LCCN 2025012895 (print) | LCCN 2025012896 (ebook) | ISBN 9798765670644 library binding | ISBN 9798348028176 paperback | ISBN 9798765691854 epub
Subjects: CYAC: Demons—Fiction | Motorcyclists—Fiction | Friendship—Fiction | LCGFT: Paranormal fiction | Novels
Classification: LCC PZ7.1.B88535 Fal 2025 (print) | LCC PZ7.1.B88535 (ebook) | DDC [Fic]—dc23/eng/20250421

LC record available at https://lccn.loc.gov/2025012895
LC ebook record available at https://lccn.loc.gov/2025012896

Manufactured in the United States of America
1 – TR – 12/15/25

To Hunter and Eloise—hunt down what makes you happy in life and don't be afraid to face your demons.

1

After the final bell rings, Liam, Madelyn, and I meet out at the soccer fields behind the school. We pretend to pay attention to the junior varsity scrimmage between the Salem Broomsticks and the Beverly Schooners. Why are we only pretending to care about the game instead of *actually* caring about it?

Well, for starters, I prefer American football to the more globally accepted European fútbol. Madelyn doesn't care for sports at all. And as for Liam, he's a demon, so human games do little to excite him. (When he explained Brimstone Ball to me, my mind was blown!)

The real reason we hang out at a lot of after-school activities is because it's great cover for what we're actually doing—planning how we're going to banish demons from our hometown of Salem, Massachusetts.

And yes, I know that I just said that Liam is a demon himself, but as best friends, we hunt alongside each other. It's really not as complicated as it sounds. We're opposites that attract, just like those mismatched animal pals you see going viral online. It also helps that Liam doesn't want to sit idly by and watch the destruction of the human race like most demons do.

Our meeting today is pretty boring. It's been quiet around Salem lately, and there hasn't been much need for our services. The frequency of strange events is way down, and things have not been going bump in the night. I don't know where the demons went, but they must be lying low.

They tend to have a hard time hiding from us because for as long as I can remember, I've been able to see and read auras. Auras are like a personal fingerprint for a soul—a living energy that surrounds the body. I can learn all sorts of things by looking at a person's aura. I can tell where you fall on the evil scale or even the last time you brushed your teeth. And let me just say, it's pretty gross how many people don't do it every day. Shame on you!

Anyway, let's just put it this way, you would have an easier time hiding things from yourself than you would from me.

It's also a skill set perfect for demon hunting because a demon's aura looks completely different from a human's, which means I can pick them out of a crowd, like picking ticks off the back of Ricky and Denise. Well, at least from the furry white half.

Ricky and Denise are two ghosts that are forced to inhabit one single earthbound cat. Each of their souls represents a different section of the feline's evenly divided body—Ricky in black fur, Denise in white. Needless to say, finding ticks on the Ricky side would be a bit more time-consuming.

Anyway, let's get back to auras. Let's take my two friends, for example. Madelyn's aura is colorful and shimmery, just like her preferred outfits. It's like catching a glimpse of an airplane in the sky when the sun is reflecting off its gleaming surface. Liam's, however, is more like a constantly twisting knot of darkness and despair. But unlike demons without any redeeming qualities, his does have the faintest hint of color. It's an inner orange glow that I call his aura's heart. It's the piece of his aura that told me he was good. Yup, it turns out two things can be true at the same time—someone can be good *and* be a trickster demon.

It was actually my mom who recognized my ability to see auras and showed me that it was a gift. She fancied herself a spiritual seeker, which meant she studied a lot of practices meant to achieve inner peace. She had read about those who could see auras and taught me that seeing an aura was not as important as reading one. An aura is a bit like a book in that respect. You can look at the pages of a book and see the words in front of you, but unless you actually read them, you won't know the *full* story. People are like that, and their auras are the pages I use to understand their intentions.

Without much to do today on the demon hunting front, our meeting ends early, and I head home from the soccer fields. Once I get inside, I go to my bedroom and sit down on the floor in front of my mom's old record player. I inherited it after she disappeared on the South American tour that *I* convinced her to go on. I like listening to her collection of vinyl through my headphones. I love the wonderful squeaks of the needle and all of the other imperfections that give vintage vinyl the kind of life you can't hear in digital music.

This collection of records is extra special, too, because it's a bit of a road map of my mom's life before I was born. During her younger days, she was a sought-after backup singer with a powerful and versatile voice. Each record in this collection features her doing some sort of background vocals for a popular artist of the time. When I listen to them now, it's a bit like I'm visiting with my mom.

For example, the tone of her voice on this folk record I just started playing reminds me of the Filipino lullabies she would whisper to me as I drifted off to sleep. I miss her so much.

The music suddenly screeches to a halt. I look up to see my dad towering over me with his six-foot-plus frame. His shoulders are so wide that sometimes he has to enter a doorway at an angle. He is still dressed in his police uniform, standing in the doorway. He's holding the cord of my headphones in his hand. They are no longer plugged into the record player.

"I've been trying to get your attention for the last two minutes," Dad says to me, sounding annoyed.

I slide the headphones down over my curly black hair and let them wrap around my neck. "Sorry. I guess I was in a daze."

My dad looks down at the record player and takes note of the album that is now silently spinning around the turntable. This particular folk record has always been his favorite of my mom's musical catalog as well. He was the one that first introduced the record to me.

His posture and tone soften.

"Got a second?" he asks me. I nod. "Good, I've got something I need to talk to you about. We both know that I give you a lot of freedom to come and go as you please, especially after school. You're a good kid, and I trust your judgment. But I have to put some restrictions on you for the time being."

I scan my memory, trying to locate something that I may have done recently to cause my dad to lock down my life. He doesn't know that I can read auras, nor does he know that I hunt demons. It isn't common knowledge that demons and other monsters walk among us, regardless of what trolls rant and rave about online. (By the way, a real troll is far less scary than an internet troll.)

My dad is great, but he's a bit of a worrywart. I'm always nervous that he's going to discover my secret and ground me until I'm eighteen. Whenever he is even the slightest bit accusatory of something I may have done, I instantly assume he's discovered my secret. If that day comes when he learns about my demon hunting, I might as well kiss any freedom I have goodbye.

He seems to sense my self-guilt and quickly assures me that these new restrictions are not of my own doing.

"Now, don't panic. This has nothing to do with you. It's just that we've got a new motorcycle gang in town, and they seem to be causing just enough trouble to keep popping up on our radar. We suspect they've got their hands in a lot of illegal stuff, but we just don't have the proof yet. We're keeping a close eye on them."

"I've heard their motorcycles," I tell him. "Yesterday on the way to school, they must have been one street over because those engines drowned out the whole bus. Liam and I had to stop talking until we got far enough away because we couldn't even hear each other."

Dad nods. "Yup. They ride these souped-up choppers—the kind of bikes with the handlebars way up here." He pretends he's riding a motorcycle with his hands stretched out in front of him at shoulder height.

I can't help but chuckle.

"This is serious. I need you to stay away from the Marquee."

"The old, abandoned movie theater that Gramps used to go to?" I ask.

"That's the one," my dad responds. "They're using that place as their new hangout. I need you to promise me that you and your friends will steer clear of there until further notice."

Having never actually been to that single-screen movie theater in my entire life, steering clear of it is not a difficult promise to make. "No problem. I'll let Liam and Madelyn know, and we'll keep our ears open for those motorcycles, too."

Motorcycle gangs are not all that common in Salem. We're more used to witches around these parts. This is, after all, where the infamous Salem Witch Trials took place way back in 1692.

Now, more than three hundred years later, the city hosts the biggest Halloween extravaganza this side of Transylvania. Every October, thousands upon thousands of spooky sightseers roll into downtown with their costumes on so that they can tour our cobblestone streets and fill up their social media feeds with what they think are pictures of ghost orbs. It's quite a boost to our economy. Somehow, I doubt a violent motorcycle gang will have the same effect.

"Good," my dad says, nodding in approval. He starts backing his way out of my bedroom but stops himself. He points down at the record that is still spinning silently. "That's a good one."

"I know," I tell him. "It's my favorite."

2

Liam and I are sprinting down a winding road that I don't think I've ever actually set foot on before. We're still in Salem, but these are the outskirts. It feels like at any moment, we could cross over into the neighboring town. But we can't stop now, and thankfully, demon hunting doesn't fall under any particular jurisdiction.

We're on the tail of a Jack Russell terrier that has been evading us for about two miles now. You see, demons don't only like to disguise themselves as humans. There is a breed of the buggers known as demon dog who, much like your own family dog, can get loose every once in a while and run away from home. Only, these putrid pups aren't fleeing from someone's backyard. They're fleeing from the home of demons, The Pit, and when they do, they tend to cause havoc wherever they go.

We caught this one peeing pure fire on an ice cream shop's fence post not far from Madelyn's house and gave chase.

"I'm . . . running . . . out of . . . breath," I wheeze to my demonic partner as he glances back at me.

"You humans are so fragile," he teases, high-stepping for dramatic effect. As a trickster demon, Liam always defaults to poking fun. "I could do this all day."

I skid to a stop, clutching my sides. "And yet . . . you still can't catch the dog either."

Before Liam can respond, the growl of illegally modified motorcycles drowns out the pitter-patter of the demon dog's overgrown toenails on the asphalt. The dog skids to a stop and turns tail, sprinting back in our direction. While it looked downright mischievous as it fled from us, now I can only see fear in the Jack Russell's expression.

"What is it doing?" Liam asks.

I think back to my dad's warning and react on instinct.

"Take cover!" I shout, diving out of the

road and shielding myself in the manicured hedges of someone's well-kept property.

With the demon dog now running directly toward him, Liam appears confused about what course of action he should take—finish the job at hand or listen to me. He very rarely does the latter.

As the sounds of motorcycles grow louder, I peek out from behind my hedge hideaway and grab Liam by his shirt. I pull my friend backward as the Jack Russell runs past us. By the time the front tire of the first motorcycle appears around the curve ahead of us, Liam and I are both tucked away inside the greenery.

Dressed in a combination of denim and leather, six burly motorcyclists scream past our bunker, the exhaust pipes of their bikes coughing up fumes that make my head spin. The sounds of their engines howl like prehistoric beasts as they pump the throttles.

The leader, a white-haired woman who looks like she could make a serious go in professional wrestling, waves the gang forward. She is older, at least from my perspective, but

I wouldn't say she is over-the-hill. If anything, she's standing on top of the hill looking down.

The group circles around the demon dog, enclosing it inside a prison of purring bike parts. The demon dog whines, something I've never heard its kind do before.

"Care to explain what we're looking at?" Liam whispers.

I shake my head, unsure of it myself. "I don't know, but their auras . . . they're not like anything I've ever seen before."

And I'm not exaggerating. Each member of the gang has an aura that is almost blinding to look at. In fact, I don't think I could stare directly at them for more than a few seconds without having to shield my eyes or look away. Instead, I try to focus on them with my peripheral vision. It's as if each aura is actually a symbol made of layers upon layers of light.

"Whatever they are, they aren't human," I quietly inform Liam.

The leader of the gang dismounts her motorcycle and turns her back to us. The leather vest she wears features an embroidered pair of angel wings with the words *The Fallen* stitched onto the material. She walks with a swagger of confidence as she inspects the demon dog with her eyes.

"Do they know what it is?" Liam asks me. I can only shrug in response.

The leader of the gang—The Fallen, I now assume—speaks directly to the demon dog. Her voice is strong and carries with it a tinny echo. "Whomever you belong to, I want you to pass along a message for me." She pauses and runs her hand through the air. A lance of pure light appears from out of nowhere. She grips it tightly. "Spread the word in The Pit that Salem is now off-limits. If they ask why, tell them it's because Iola says so!"

The demon dog whimpers as Iola drives the lance of light downward, piercing the demon dog's soul. Its disguise falters, turning to ash and then blowing away on the gentle breeze that passes by. Beneath its coating of fur is its true form—a three-headed monstrosity, each with a forked tongue hanging from its mouth. Its appearance is far more like a fuzzy-faced Komodo dragon than a cute and cuddly Jack Russell.

Iola retracts the lance and the demon dog implodes, returning to the depths of its unholy origin.

Liam and I remain quiet, but we turn to each other as an understanding hits us both at the same time. Everything we thought we knew about demon hunting has just been altered forever.

3

Night eventually rolls around, and I can't sleep a wink. That's fine by me because I have to talk about what I saw, and the only one I can think to do that with is my very own parasitic paralysis demon, Boo-en.

Paralysis demons feed off of humans as they sleep. I never knew that they existed until I woke up with one using me as his own personal all-you-can-eat buffet. Because I am quite familiar with all sorts of demonic entities, I wasn't exactly surprised when I opened my eyes in the middle of Boo-en siphoning off my physical energy. That's a paralysis demon's favorite meal—you know, the stuff that allows a person to wake up in the morning with that get-up-and-go energy.

Anyone who wakes up feeling like they need a nap is probably being visited by a paralysis demon while they're sleeping. These people tend to have no idea the demon has been using them as a pit stop between two worlds. Instead, they blame their lack of energy on a restless night's sleep.

As for Boo-en and me, we kind of hit it off immediately. We started chatting, and before I knew it, it was morning. He has never been all that comfortable being a demon and prefers the company of humans. The next night, he returned, and it was more of the same—we talked about everything from sneaker collections to the meaning of life.

Now, we have what we like to call a gentleman's agreement. I allow him to pop into my room every night so that he can feed, and he promises to read from the nonfiction books I leave out. I've heard that the unconscious brain can absorb knowledge even while you sleep, and I like the idea of being able to use my time in multiple ways. I have a biography on the life of English philosopher Francis Bacon on my nightstand, but it's going to stay closed tonight.

I feel the hair on the back of my neck working feverishly to stand to attention. A surge of energy circulates through my bedroom, and I know that Boo-en is almost here. I listen closely as the familiar sound of a *pop, pop, POP* trickles down from above. It's like someone is sprinkling candy down onto me—the kind that fizzles when you pour it into your mouth. The air suddenly smells sugary, which only makes me think of more sweets.

Flash!

A doorway between our world and The Pit opens up a few feet above my bed. Boo-en sticks his head in, and his pebble-like pupils sharpen. He's surprised to find me staring up at him.

"Boo-en is early?" he asks. He's used to finding me asleep at this time of night.

I sit up. "No, you're good. I was just hoping we could change up the routine tonight and talk for a bit."

Boo-en hesitates. He continues to stare down from the portal.

"Don't worry, you can still eat," I assure him.

A smile stretches across Boo-en's face, and he drops down from the portal, diving headfirst into my mattress. Looking like a cross between a prehistoric weasel and a modern-day llama, he rubs his jaw—underbite and all—over my blankets, marking his territory with his demonic pheromones.

"Why do you always have to do that?" I ask.

Boo-en pops upright, sitting in a way that completely mirrors my own. "Boo-en's scent tells other paralysis demons not to eat here. Damon belongs to Boo-en."

I pull my blanket up to my nose and sniff it. It smells like a blueberry muffin if you replaced the blueberries with rotten eggs. "Ugh. My dad keeps buying me new deodorant because he thinks I have terrible body odor, thanks to you."

Boo-en smiles. "Damon welcome!" He has mistaken my insult for a compliment. "Now, what Damon want to talk to Boo-en about?"

I can feel myself getting more and more physically exhausted with each passing second that Boo-en is here. That's the funny thing about paralysis demons; you can't see them feeding on your energy, but you sure can feel it.

"I saw something yesterday," I tell him. "A kind of aura that I have never seen before. It was like these people had a spotlight over their heads, and inside each one of their auras, I could see some kind of symbol."

Boo-en's body contorts in on itself. He looks troubled. "What kind of symbol did Damon see?"

I struggle to properly describe the symbols. I was only able to see them out of the corner of my eye. All I can manage to tell Boo-en is that they were made of light, comprised of only straight lines, and that they seemed to change their shape based on how the person was standing.

Boo-en holds up one of his hands, which is clenched in a fist so tightly that his knuckles have turned white. He uncurls his unnaturally long fingers and traces something in the air between us.

"Damon must close eyes," he tells me. I do as I'm told. "Damon must *not* look at the spot where Boo-en draw."

Demons often talk in riddles. It's in their nature to be obtuse and to cause confusion in the human world, even when they don't mean to. I've known Boo-en long enough to be able to decipher the less straightforward things he says. In this case, I'm pretty sure he's asking me to look at the space between us with my eyes closed. I turn my head to face the area in question and see a familiar symbol etched into the darkness, glowing like a beacon in my mind.

My eyes open. "That's it," I tell him, confirming that what I *didn't* just see is, in fact, what I actually saw in the auras of The Fallen. "What is it? What are they?"

Boo-en swallows so hard that his neck elongates like a goose when it ruffles its feathers. "Demons like Boo-en are taught from a young age to stay far away from those that Damon saw. Damon should not interact. Damon should ignore. Stay far away."

"Enough with the dramatics," I tell Boo-en. "Just tell me what they are!"

He leans in close and whispers as if saying the name out loud will bring the sky itself down onto him. "Damon saw angels."

It's Saturday morning, and I'm standing in the parking lot of our local library with a belly full of cereal. Liam is with me, and Madelyn is inside on standby, ready to assist us from afar should we need access to any information while we work.

"Didn't your dad tell us specifically to avoid this place at all costs?" Liam asks me. My trickster BFF is uneasy, which is not something I'm used to seeing.

I glance out over the library's parking lot and across the busy downtown street toward the brick building that was once a popular stop for moviegoers. The Marquee hasn't been open to the public for as long as I've been alive, but from what my grandpa used to tell me, it was quite the hot spot in its day. There isn't much of a need for a single-screen movie theater today, though. Not when there's a sixteen-screen cinema with a state-of-the-art surround sound system and reclining seats less than a mile away.

"He did," I confirm to Liam. "But these are angels we're talking about. They're the good guys. He only told me to stay away because he thought they were a bunch of baddies causing trouble."

Liam shifts uncomfortably. "For you, they may be the good guys, but I'm public enemy number one as far as they're concerned. Besides, haven't you ever heard of never judging a book by its cover? How do you know they're not causing trouble?"

I think about this for a moment. I saw them smite that demon dog with my own eyes. Whatever they're up to, we're obviously on the same team.

Liam is right about one thing, though. They probably won't take too kindly to him being a demon, so it's best that he hang back while I head over and introduce myself.

"You stay here," I tell him. "We don't need

you accidentally getting smote."

I start to move forward, but Liam grabs hold of my shoulder, stopping me from leaving. It's easy enough for him to stop me. Liam is tall and imposing, much larger than the rest of the kids in our grade. He could easily pass for a senior if it wasn't for his baby face. I, on the other hand, could not.

"Not so fast," he says. "You can't just walk in there and tell them that you're part of some local, independent demon hunting group. You saw what kind of weapons they're packing. Do you really think a lance of pure light won't work on a human just as well as it does a demon?"

I sidestep Liam's grasp on me and put a few feet of space between us.

"I'm sure it can, but they have no reason to use it on me. To be honest, I'd really like the chance to talk about demon hunting with someone who may actually know a thing or two about it. Everything we know, we have had to teach ourselves. This is our opportunity to really learn about our craft from those who have been doing it for . . . centuries? Yeah, probably centuries. Angels can give us the kind of knowledge that can guarantee Salem's safety. It's a win, Liam. It's a win for all of us."

Liam reluctantly eases up, burying his tension deep within himself. "Fine. Go ahead. Go introduce yourself to the halos, but I'm going to be right here just in case it goes bad. You shout, and I'll be in that theater in less than thirty seconds."

I smile a toothy grin in appreciation. It's nice to know that Liam always has my back, even if he disagrees. Not only is he a good friend, but, thankfully for me, he's also insanely strong because of the demon blood pumping through his veins.

I once saw him stop a city bus to save a raccoon that had chosen the worst possible time to cross the street. Liam grabbed the rear bumper of the bus and just held it in place long enough for the raccoon to scurry into the underbrush and disappear out of sight. It was impressive.

I wait for a lull in traffic and then run

across the street, stopping at the steps that lead up to the Marquee.

I never really noticed it before, probably because I never took the time to look, but the building has a lot of charm. It reminds me of the kind of place you'd see represented in those miniature villages that pop up in craft stores around the holidays.

I half expect it to be made of ceramic as I make my way up the stairs, not wanting to linger out front any longer than I need to. If my dad spots me here, I'll need more than an angel to save me.

The two large wooden doors of the Marquee seem about as thick as the bricks that make up the exterior. Someone would have to be literally standing on the other side of the doors to hear my knocking. So, instead, I ignore the *No Trespassing* signs hanging in the windows and check the doors to see if they're unlocked. Both swing outward with ease, and I slip inside before anyone can tell me otherwise.

The lobby is big and spacious, with a

ceiling that seems to have been built for giraffes. Every inch of the walls is adorned with a combination of red felt curtains and ornately carved pillars, their sculpted golden vines stretching up toward the ceiling. The air is dank and humid, but a faint hint of stale popcorn still wafts through the Marquee's interior.

I feel my cell phone vibrate in my pocket and fish it out. It's Madelyn.

"What's up?" I ask as I answer her call.

"I've been doing a bit of research online, Damon. Funny thing is, I keep coming across a lot of lore that suggests angels aren't as warm and fuzzy as they're made out to be in the movies." I immediately sense the worry in Madelyn's voice. "I don't know if this is such a good idea."

"I appreciate the heads up. I'll be careful, but they can't possibly be as bad as the demons we've faced. I'll call you after."

I hang up the phone before Madelyn can respond and then move through the lobby cautiously. Regardless of what Madelyn's research suggests, I don't fear the angels. But I also don't want to catch any of them by surprise. An accidental smiting is no way to leave this world.

"Hello?" I call out as I near the room where the movie screen once hung. The doors have been partially propped open with a wooden wedge.

I inch closer to the crack in the doors and catch a hint of light coming from within.

"Is there anyone here?" I reach out and grab the metal handle. It's warm to the touch, and I receive the most intense static shock of my life.

"I'm coming in," I announce as I open the doors to the theater. "I mean no harm."

Inside, rows and rows of dilapidated theater seats stretch downward on a slight slope to where the movie screen was once suspended. Now, in its place, the same symbol seen on the back of The Fallen's leather vests has been etched onto the wall in what appears to be ash and soot.

Below the graffiti, hunched over a steel

barrel that spits flames of a supernatural blue hue, Iola stares at me.

"You may mean no harm, human, but harm may come to you," she says ominously.

5

I hold my hands out in front of me and make my way down the aisle. Iola doesn't bother to move from the spot she's standing in, but she also doesn't take her bright blue eyes off me. I'm sensing some serious trust issues.

"My name is Damon," I offer without her asking for it. "I hunt demons."

If I've impressed Iola with my knowledge of the supernatural, she doesn't show it. Instead, she lifts her nose in the air and inhales deeply.

"You're human. That much is obvious," she concludes. "But you reek of demon swine."

"I . . . I have an ally," I mumble, already regretting my decision to enter the Marquee. "A friend."

As I get closer to Iola, I have to turn away from her. Her aura stings my retinas, causing my eyes to water. I stop my march down the aisle halfway between the doors and Iola. I instinctively know that if I move any closer, her aura could cause serious and lasting damage to my vision.

"I can read auras," I tell her.

She scoffs. "And why on this world that He created would you even think that I'd care?"

I bring my right arm up to my face, shielding as much of her blazing aura as I can. I question why I came here after all. Why did I not just listen to Liam and Madelyn's concerns?

"I was hunting the demon dog your gang took care of yesterday. I saw you send it back to where it came from. I thought we could . . . I don't know, work together?"

Iola laughs, and the sound echoes in my skull as if it were amplified by the world's most powerful speakers.

The cackle causes me to lose my balance, and I'm forced to collapse into the nearest theater seat, which rattles as it accepts the first weight it's caught in decades. It feels like someone has whacked a gong just behind my eye sockets, and the vibrations have completely zapped my ability to think clearly. I clutch at my head, hoping the laughter will stop. After a few seconds, it does. But those seconds feel like minutes inside my mind.

"Foolish human dog," Iola says, amused by the discomfort that her laughter is causing me. "You assume too much and know too little. I have absolutely zero interest in the war you claim to wage. I destroyed that demon dog because it wandered into The Fallen's turf, plain and simple."

I pull myself up to my feet. I try to steady myself. "Turf?"

"Mm-hmm," she continues, stepping around the steel barrel and forcing me back up the aisle to keep a safe distance from her aura. "The World Above was our turf until we got tossed out on our butts. Was it justified? Sure! It is, after all, the cost of sinning in His presence. In fact, that's where my fellow Fallen are right now—out on the streets, living it up like His deplorable humans. It's lucky for us that we prefer being down here with you walking meat puppets, wouldn't you say? This way, we can sin as much as we want."

The gong goes off inside my head again as Iola releases another cackle. I can't sit this time, though. She makes her way up the aisle, keeping me on my heels and forcing me backward. I stumble but manage to stay upright.

"But you're supposed to be the good guys," I declare. I understand how silly it sounds coming out of my mouth given the current situation. But I can't help but cling to the idea I've held on to for so long.

Iola waves a finger at me, showing disappointment in my naivete. She mocks me, and I feel myself begin to sweat. I really wish I hadn't come in here alone.

"Yes, and the demons are meant to be the bad." She sniffs at the air again as if to prove her point. "And yet you fraternize with one so closely."

"He's not like the others," I remark.

"And neither are we—like the other angels," she declares. "You clearly know that this world exists outside the parameters of only two pillars of judgment. A world that is black and white is a world for the predictable and the expendable. I'm something else. Myself and my Fallen—we reside in the gray."

"But . . ."

A fiendish grin stretches across Iola's face. "And the gray has now come home to roost. So spread the word. Salem belongs to The Fallen now."

Iola snaps her fingers, and I suddenly find myself standing on the steps outside of the Marquee, having no idea how I got there. I remain frozen and stunned as Liam appears alongside me, looking every bit as confused as I feel.

"What just happened?" he asks. "I was staring at the theater from across the street, and then *POOF*, you were just standing here all of a sudden. The door never opened."

I slowly turn my head to look at Liam. His expression becomes sour—like he's sucking on the world's sourest lemon—as he weighs the seriousness of my fight-or-flight face.

"We've got a big problem," I say, still hearing Iola's residual laughter ringing through the recesses of my now terrified mind.

I really don't want to hear his 'I-told-you-so,' but I suppose there is no avoiding it now. "The angels aren't playing nice. All they care about are themselves. And worst of all . . . I think I just made them mad."

Madelyn meets Liam and me outside the café where I like to get an occasional Persian-style iced tea. From there, the three of us start walking back to my house. My dad is on duty all day, so we have the place to ourselves to figure out what to do about The Fallen.

"And you're sure they're angels?" Madelyn asks, shifting the umbrella she's holding in her hands so that it blocks out every bit of the sun. She was born with albinism, and her fair skin is extremely sensitive to the UV rays raining down from above.

Madelyn learned about my aura-reading ability when I tumbled into her one afternoon. I was in the middle of wrestling a nightmare demon—small, but feisty creatures—and Madelyn didn't even have to think twice. She helped me get control over it long enough so that I could give it a holy water shower. We've been friends ever since.

"I'm sure," I tell her. "Not only did Boo-en identify their auras immediately when I described them, but the leader, Iola, told me they had been kicked out of The World Above for sinning. They are all angels."

Madelyn finds all of this information to be about as shocking as if I told her it was Saturday. Which is to say, not shocking at all because it *is* Saturday. Our abnormal lifestyles have pretty much made us numb to the kind of news that would cause most jaws to drop in any other friend group.

I make a mental note that we really need to make it a point to do some ordinary, run-of-the-mill teenager stuff after this angel business is over with.

"It also lines up with their gang name," Liam offers. "They're fallen angels, and they ride under the flag of The Fallen."

I nod. "It's a little on the nose, but based on my chat with their leader, angels don't seem all that big on subtlety."

Liam cracks his thick knuckles, popping each one down the line as he presses the backs of his hands against his jaw.

"So, how do we stop them?" he asks.

"I'm not sure we can," I reply, though I wish I could say something more uplifting. "I couldn't even look directly at Iola when I got close to her. It felt like her aura would burn the eyes right out of my skull if I did. She's easily the most powerful being I've ever been around."

Madelyn stops in the shade of a towering oak tree and turns to face Liam and me. We're less than two blocks away from my house. "Well, while you two were at the Marquee, I decided to do a little preemptive research on angels, which I mentioned briefly to Damon. While most of what you can find online about them is about miracles or written as fantastical fan fiction, I was able to dig up some old religious texts that specifically reference angels who walk the Earth. I think you'll find one passage particularly interesting."

Madelyn closes her umbrella and leans it

against the trunk of the tree before she tucks her long, white-blond hair behind her ears. She reaches into her pocket and pulls out a piece of paper, unfolding it to reveal the translated words. She reads:

"... for those who walk amongst His children do so without their wings. To return to The World Above without His invitation is not an option, lest their wings be doused in holy oil and set ablaze. This surrenders their status as the chosen few and returns their souls to the majority."

"Okay," I say. "It's interesting, sure. But why is it important?"

Madelyn breaks the translation down even further for us. "Any fallen angels need to be invited back into The World Above, otherwise they stay here on Earth. However, they would stop being angels altogether if we were to burn their wings with holy oil. That's how we beat them."

Liam cocks his head to the side. "So, let me get this straight. We have to not only find some genuine holy oil, but then we have to find their wings, which, last I checked, weren't on their backs—only to burn said wings in a divine bonfire?"

Madelyn gestures down to the printout in her hand. "If you believe this ancient text."

"I don't believe *any* of this," Liam says, capping it off with a sigh.

As my mind wanders on the topic of angels, I catch a glimpse of a furry four-legged something out of the corner of my eye. I turn to face it and realize that it's the stray cat containing two earthbound souls.

Ricky and Denise, the spirits who now inhabit the feline, were teenage boyfriend and girlfriend back when they were alive in the 1950s. When someone challenged Ricky to a drag race, he accepted, even though Denise was in the passenger seat next to him. Things were going Ricky's way, too—he was winning the race and embarrassing his rival—until a cat crossed in front of his Chevy, causing Ricky to yank the steering wheel to the side. There was no time to brake, and Ricky wrapped his car around a tree.

The same tree that we are now standing under.

Ricky and Denise were killed instantly that night, and the star-crossed lovers have been stuck in that cat ever since.

"What do you want, Ricky and Denise?" I ask with a purposeful tone of annoyance. "I don't have any food on me if that's what you're looking for."

They stop at my feet and rub up against my legs. This sign of affection always makes me uncomfortable, knowing that the cat is being controlled by two humans. "Be cool, Daddy-O," Ricky purrs. I know it's Ricky because he speaks out of the left, black side of the cat's mouth. "I just thought you'd want to be hip to the fact that the heat is parked outside your pad."

Ricky talks like someone from a poorly made period piece movie. Although he's been haunting Salem for more than seventy years, he still uses slang ripped from the 1950s.

"If you're talking about a cop car," I say, deciphering Ricky's use of the term *heat*, "yeah, my dad is a cop, remember? There's usually one parked in my driveway."

"This is not your father, though," Denise responds. I know it's her because she talks out of the right, white side of the cat's mouth. "These are two other police officers. And they look distressed."

I take off running. I don't stop to tell my friends that I'll meet them back at my house. They both know that the last time there were police officers waiting in my driveway, it was to tell my dad and me that Mom was missing. Needless to say, that was the worst day of my life. I just hope this doesn't mean I'm about to have an even worse one.

As I round the corner of my street, I spot the squad car in question. I immediately know it's not my dad's. I recognize the officer in the passenger seat right away. It's Omar Acosta, a close friend of my dad's. He's been by the house numerous times for cookouts and holidays. He even made his famous chili dip for last year's Super Bowl party.

He spots me slowing to a jog as I near the

driveway, and he climbs out of the police car.

"Heya, Damon," he says, putting way too much sympathy into just those two words. I feel my stomach sink toward the ground.

"What happened?" I ask, knowing already that something did.

Officer Acosta takes off his hat and looks somber as he rubs his hand through his thinning hair. "It's your pops . . . he's been injured."

7

Liam and Madelyn are right behind me, so Officer Acosta and his partner wait for me to quickly fill my friends in on what happened before they drive me over to the hospital. As far as they know, Dad's in stable condition, but he took a pretty bad beating so the doctors were worried that he might have brain bleeding. The last Officer Acosta heard, Dad was going in to have a CT scan.

"Who did it?" I ask, my teeth grinding together so aggressively that I can feel myself getting a headache.

Officer Acosta turns around in his seat to face me. "I don't think your pops would be too keen on me telling you that kind of information."

I want the answer, but deep down, I already know who is responsible. "The Fallen?"

Officer Acosta's face twitches ever so slightly, the smallest of tells that would probably go completely overlooked at a poker table. More importantly, however, his aura—a flowery bouquet of oranges and yellows—flares as if it were struck by a surge of electricity.

You can disguise a face, but you can never disguise an aura.

"I don't know what you're referring to, Damon," he says, turning himself back around. "Besides, we're here."

Officer Acosta offers to accompany me into the hospital, but I decline. He and his partner tell me that they'll wait outside in the parking lot, and then when I'm done visiting with my dad, they'll give me a ride home. I thank them both and head inside.

After checking in at numerous desks, I'm eventually directed through a large set of doors. There, a nurse tells me I can find my dad behind the curtains marked Triage 3. As I stand in front of the thin cotton barrier of the curtain, I hear the steady pinging of a monitor coming from the other side.

Beep. Beep. Beep.

At least his heart sounds healthy.

"Dad?" I say quietly, hopeful for a positive response.

"Damon?" his familiar, deep baritone of a voice booms out from the other side of the curtain. "I wasn't looking forward to you seeing me like this, but I don't suppose I can hide it forever. Come on in."

I slide the curtain open on its overhead rings and step inside the improvised room. Had he not spoken to me, I would've had a difficult time recognizing the man lying in the hospital bed.

My dad's face is so swollen and bruised that he reminds me of one of the Halloween decorations we set up in our front yard every October. (When you live in the horror capital of the United States, you have to play the part.)

He has a pencil-length cut across his dark forehead with fresh sutures holding it closed, each visible stitch looking like the legs of a nasty horsefly trying to escape its fleshy prison. His right eye is so puffed up that it is nearly closed, and his front tooth has been chipped down to half its regular size.

It's hard to look at my dad without wanting to cry.

"You should see the other guy," he jokingly states. If he's smiling beneath all the swelling, I can't tell.

I step up to my dad's bed and rest my hand on his knee. "How did this happen?"

He looks away. He appears embarrassed by the question—or at least the answer to the question.

"It doesn't matter how much training you have. Sometimes, the person you're up against is just one step faster than you or one step ahead of you. And that's life in a nutshell, Damon. You don't win every race you set out to run. It's how you handle the losses—how you move beyond them—that matters."

I stand there in silence. I'm experiencing so many different emotions at once that I don't know which one to focus on. I don't know what feeling to bring to the surface.

"Hey," my dad continues, taking advantage

of the quiet moment. "I've been meaning to tell you how proud of you I am."

I look up from my own internal conflict and lock eyes with my dad. I can see his aura shining just beyond my peripheral vision—a rich ball of purple that constantly turns in on itself as if you're looking through a toy kaleidoscope. "What do you mean?"

"Well, seeing you listen to your mom's old records—I just think that it's something she'd really appreciate, you know? You're holding onto her memory, and you're doing it in a way that helps keep her alive. I love that . . . and I love you."

I struggle to reciprocate the warm and fuzzy feelings my dad is showering me with. Instead, I remain focused on the *how*. *How* did this happen? *How* did my father end up lying in a hospital bed?

"That gang—The Fallen—did they do this?" I ask.

"None of that matters," he says, waving me in for a hug. I embrace him, squeezing lightly so as not to put any extra pressure on his injuries. "I'm going to be okay, and the rest of my brothers and sisters in blue are going to bring the responsible parties to justice. I'm just glad you're here now. I'm glad we have each other."

Dad can say that it doesn't matter to him, but it matters to me. Iola and her crew just made a big mistake because they came after my family. They made it personal. Now, I don't care if they go back up to The World Above or down to The Pit, but one way or another, I'm going to make sure that The Fallen are evicted from Salem.

8

"So, let me get this straight, Daddy-O," Ricky says the next day as Madelyn places a special collar around the cat's neck. "You want me and my girl to sneak into the theater and eyeball our way around until we find some angel wings? Am I diggin' that right?"

Madelyn, Liam, and I are back at the library parking lot across from the Marquee. I stayed at Liam's house last night because Dad had to be kept at the hospital overnight for observation. Thankfully, it's Sunday morning now, so the library is closed, and we have the parking lot to ourselves. That's a big benefit to us because we're having a conversation with a literal talking cat, and that's something people tend to notice.

"That's right," I tell Ricky. "The Marquee is The Fallen's hideout, so we assume the wings are being kept somewhere inside. We just need you to tell us where, and we'll handle the rest."

Madelyn adjusts the collar until she finds a position on the cat's neck that works with the technology she's equipped it with. "I installed a tiny camera in the collar that will stream directly onto my phone. We'll be able to see what you see when you see it."

Ricky and Denise turn to face the Marquee. The right side of the cat's mouth opens, and Denise speaks. "Ricky and I used to come here all the time when we were . . . well, you know. On Sundays, they'd run a double feature matinee—the really low-budget science fiction movies with actors in foam suits. We'd spend hours in there together."

The cat nods, and Ricky joins in. "Can't say we saw many boss flicks, but we did make some boss memories."

"So then, you know your way around the place?" Liam asks.

"Yeah," Ricky responds, a hint of sadness present in his voice. "We got this. But just so

I'm hip with the plan, what do we do if we actually come face-to-face with any of the angels?"

I kneel down and look at them in their reflective green eyes. "Run!"

Five minutes later, Liam and I are huddled over Madelyn's shoulders looking down at the phone in her hands. We can see what Ricky and Denise see, their journey playing out on the screen. First, they cross the street. Then, they circle the perimeter of the Marquee in search of an entry point. They find one in a lower-level window where the right corner of the glass has shattered. They slip through the hole with ease.

"Can we communicate with them?" I ask.

Madelyn shakes her head. "No. They won't be able to hear us, but we will be able to hear them."

On the screen, Ricky and Denise emerge from the shadows and step into what looks like the theater's dusty basement. Forgotten boxes of supplies are buried beneath cobwebs and mouse poop. There is no sign that anyone has been down there for years. And there certainly aren't any angel wings lying around.

After locating the stairs, the pair trots up and pops out into a small manager's office. There's still a desk and a chair in the room, but that's about it. From there, Ricky and Denise push their way out of the office through the closed door and end up in the lobby.

"Oh, Ricky," we hear Denise say. "It looks identical to how it did when we'd come here on our dates."

They sprint across the lobby to the theater. "Don't sweat it, babe," Ricky comforts Denise. "We may not have the Marquee no more, but we still have each other. For eternity, too. Not many folks can say that."

Ricky and Denise squeeze through the partially open theater doors and then quickly conceal themselves beneath a row of seats. They have to sidestep a wad of decades-old bubble gum that remains stuck to the floor before rising up from the row of seats and cautiously surveying the room.

Although there are no angels present, the

strange fire continues to burn inside the steel barrel.

"That was burning the last time I was here," I tell my friends, finding it odd that the fire hasn't burned itself out yet.

Madelyn brings the screen up to her eyes and investigates the fire more closely.

"Ugh," Denise moans, her voice unsteady as it comes through the cell phone's speaker. "I don't know what it is, but being near that fire is zapping every bit of energy I have. We need to get away from it."

Ricky and Denise turn to scan the wall at their back. They focus in on a two-foot by two-foot window, which looks in on the projector room. That's where the projectionist once ran the movie reels through a machine that showed the films on the screen for the audience to see.

"I think that fire is fueled by holy oil," Madelyn says. This takes both Liam and me by surprise.

"What makes you think that?" Liam asks.

As Ricky and Denise search for a way to

access the projector room, our eyes remain transfixed on the screen.

"Well," Madelyn continues, "the flame's blue hue is not a normal indicator of a natural temperature. It also seems to be affecting Ricky and Denise, which makes sense because they are spirits, after all."

"So?" Liam blurts out, unclear of the connection.

Madelyn clarifies. "Holy oil is an ingredient used in exorcisms. An exorcism is an extremely complicated ritual that can remove spirits from the bodies of those they possess. A regular fire wouldn't have any impact on Ricky and Denise at all."

"Question," I begin, trying to make sense of everything I'm hearing. "Why would the angels create a fire made from the very oil that can destroy them?"

Madelyn nods, expecting the question. "It's an eternal flame. That holy oil will continue to burn for as long as they use the location as their home. Without their wings, the angels need a source of power. The eternal flame is it."

As we quietly celebrate our luck, thankful to the fallen angels for embracing the very thing capable of turning them mortal, Ricky and Denise locate a small door that leads to the projector room. They scamper up the stairs and strategically use one of their paws to nudge the door open. Inside, piled up on the dusty ground, there are half a dozen pairs of snow-white angel wings looking like someone's discarded laundry.

"Jackpot!" I say. "We have everything we need!"

"I'm going in to finish this," I announce, breaking away from Madelyn's phone.

Liam places his hand on my chest. His demonic strength keeps me from moving any farther. "Not so fast, Damon. The theater seems angel-free right now, but we don't know where they are or when they're coming back."

I look down at Liam's hand, willing him to remove it. He doesn't. "Yeah, and we also don't know if we'll get another chance like this again, so I'm taking it!"

"Then I'm coming in with you," he tells me.

I shake my head. "No way. Iola could smell you on me even when you weren't standing right beside me. For all we know, they've got some kind of demon security system that will alert them to your arrival as soon as you step foot in the place. Remember, they're all about protecting their turf. We can't risk it."

"I agree with Damon," Madelyn states. "We can keep watch from out here so long as you stick by Ricky and Denise."

Liam retracts his hand and stands down. "Fine, but if any feathers start flying in there, I'm coming in and throwing punches first, asking questions second."

I agree to Liam's terms, mostly because I have no interest in going toe-to-toe with an angel by myself. There's no point in establishing any sort of signal with Liam and Madelyn either because even inside the Marquee, I'll hear The Fallen's motorcycles before I can hear any sort of alert from my friends. From here on out, our success hinges on Iola and her crew staying busy elsewhere.

Ricky and Denise meet me at the front doors, and I ask them to follow me in so that Liam and Madelyn can keep track of my progress. They agree, and together, we make our way up to the projector room.

The air inside the projector room is laced with a mixture of fruity scents—a sort of hybrid of grapefruit and cranberry. The closer I get to the wings, the stronger the aroma gets. It's actually quite intoxicating.

I point to a spot for Ricky and Denise to position themselves as I ready myself to lift the wings. "Stand over here so your camera can watch my back as I pick these up and take them out of here."

They do as I ask. I kneel down to pick up the wings, but I can't budge the pile in the slightest. Even though they look as light as the feathers they're made of, the wings are exceptionally heavy. Each one must weigh at least one hundred pounds.

"What's the sitch, Daddy-O?" Ricky asks.

I glance around the room, looking for an alternative plan. "I can't carry them. They're too heavy. Dragging each one down the stairs would take too long."

"Did you bring the holy oil?" Denise asks out of the right side of the cat's mouth.

I point down into the theater through the small projector room window. "Madelyn thinks that's what's burning in the barrel. I just need to get the wings from here to there."

Looking at the projector room window gives me an idea. I rush over to it and grab hold of the shoddy wooden frame. It's splintered and barely holding onto the wall as it is, making it easy to tear from its mounting. I toss the frame aside and then ball my hand into a fist. I punch the glass firmly, and it falls from its housing, shattering onto the theater floor below.

I go back to the mass of wings and drag one from the pile. My muscles strain as I pull it toward the opening in the projector room wall. Although extremely heavy, the wings are also spectacularly malleable. I'm able to reshape it into a ball and push it out through the opening. It smashes down to the theater floor, taking out a row of seats as it does.

One individual wing down, eleven to go.

Already sweating, I turn back to the pile and feel the hairs on my arms stand on end. The pile of wings shakes and shimmies, and then something—*someone*—rises up from the heap of feathers.

I turn to Ricky and Denise to tell them to

abort the mission and leave the Marquee, but they're already fleeing the room. So much for the possessed cat having my back. I guess that's yet another reason to officially label myself a dog person.

"Fun fact about angels," I hear Iola's voice declare as she ascends into the air above the feathers. "Angels can still feel it when you touch their disconnected wings. We are forever connected to them."

With Iola's aura now on full display and only inches from my face, it feels like the inside of my skull is on fire. Even with my eyes closed, the brilliance of her aura is visible to me. I know that if she wanted to, she could incinerate the eyes from my head with a single thought.

For once, I wish I had actually listened to my dad and stayed away from the Marquee.

10

Iola floats down until the soles of her riding boots touch the floor. I feel her aura dim, and the scorching pain inside my head lessens enough that I can at least now pay attention to what is happening.

"Open your eyes, human dog," she demands of me. "I want you to witness the fate that awaits you."

I slowly open my eyes. Apparently, angels can control their auras because Iola has all but turned hers off. You learn something new every day, I guess. I just wish I would live long enough to file that information away for later use.

She stares daggers through me.

"I thought I made it clear that I would not tolerate anyone complicating the affairs of The Fallen. And yet here you are, your pathetic human paw caught red-handed in my cookie jar."

I'm not sure how I'm going to get out of this alive, but I know that I can't talk my way out of it.

"Here's how I suggest we mend the damage to our unsalvageable relationship," Iola sarcastically says. "First, I kill you. Right here, right now. And then, I kill everyone that you know and love, starting with that punching bag of a father of yours. I think that, combined with my forgiving nature, would bring us to a good place that I could be happy with. What about you?"

I glance toward the door, wondering if I can make it out before Iola smites me down.

"You can't," she answers. I don't know if she was able to read my mind or read my face, but it doesn't matter. I'm dead where I stand.

Or so I think.

The screeching howl of an angry cat pierces the silence as Ricky and Denise leap in from the open doorway, latching onto the back of Iola's head. They sink their claws into her skull and hold on for dear life.

I take it all back. I'm totally, 100 percent a cat person!

The wall at Iola's back explodes inward, creating a blizzard of drywall dust that clouds my vision.

Thankfully, I am still able to see enough of the action play out as Liam bursts into the room, tackling Iola from behind and taking the angel by surprise. The pair—along with one clingy cat—continues forward and crashes through the opposite wall, wrestling in midair as they fall down into the theater below.

"Liam!" I shout, worried about my friend's safety.

I look down into the theater from the newly formed, angel-sized hole in the wall. Liam flings Iola through the air, causing her body to rip three rows of theater chairs from their bolted position.

Wooden armrests and flimsy cushions are dispersed chaotically about. Ricky and Denise detach themselves from Iola's head and flee from the theater. I'm thankful for their distraction and will let them know, should I survive this entire ordeal.

"Don't worry about me!" Liam shouts. "I'll keep the holier-than-thou biker busy while you finish the job."

Iola rises to her feet. Her eyes spark with electricity. "The only thing that will be finished here today is your existence, demon swine."

Knowing that time is of the essence, I start dragging the angel wings to the hole in the wall—one by one—and toss them down into the theater.

Each time I look out on the battle taking place between Iola and Liam, my best friend appears one step closer to having his keister kicked. By the fifth trip to the hole in the wall, Iola has him by the throat, mocking what "little time" he has left alive.

I have to do something to help him.

I reach into my pocket and pull out a jagged hunk of bright green malachite. The somewhat rare copper carbonate mineral is an open line to The Pit, allowing me to contact Boo-en whenever I want to. It's basically a supernatural cell phone.

"Damon to Boo-en," I say into the malachite as I hold it up to my mouth. "We desperately need your help up here. Please respond."

The rock glows, signaling that Boo-en has received my message. Whether he wants to reply or not is another matter altogether.

"Boo-en?" I ask again. "Please!"

The malachite glows a second time, only now it's followed by Boo-en's hollow voice, which seems to come directly from the rock. Or at least, from somewhere within it.

"Boo-en know better than to anger angels."

I clutch the rock tightly and speak firmly into it. "If you don't help us, we're goners. Now, I estimate Liam has about ten more seconds of life left before he's dead. After that, it's my turn. So gosh darn it, Boo-en—DO SOMETHING!"

Silence follows the glow. I've all but given up when Boo-en finally decides to get involved.

"Boo-en have friend that owes Boo-en favor," he says through the malachite. "Damon throw rock at angel's feet and Boo-en do the rest."

Without having to be told the instructions a second time, I hurl the malachite down into the melee. It hits the theater floor and then rolls down the aisle, skidding to a stop at Iola's riding boots. She looks down at it, puzzled. She has no better idea than I do about what is about to happen.

"My goodness, you humans have terrible aim," she says, assuming I had meant to throw the rock *at* her. "Not that your little rock would have hurt me."

The malachite flattens out like a pancake and becomes an active portal to another world.

"Damon and Liam shield eyes," Boo-en's voice calls out from inside the phantom doorway. "Some horrors a human and his trickster pal cannot unsee."

Unfortunately, curiosity gets the better of me, and I keep my eyes open.

Giant lime-green tentacles slither out of the portal and wrap around Iola, tethering her in place.

The undersides of the tentacles are lined with thousands of active eyeballs, which constantly survey the room as if looking for an item of significance or hoping to hear praise for a job well done. If it's the latter, I'm too bowled over by what I'm witnessing to give it what it needs.

"Boo-en told you not to look at friend who owes Boo-en favor!"

11

Liam drags himself away from the entangled Iola. He looks up to the hole in the projector room wall, which frames me in a jagged jumble of broken plaster.

"I need your help!" I shout. "These wings are way heavier than they look!"

Liam glances back at Iola. The demonic tentacles constrict like a nest of anacondas, making it impossible for the angel to speak.

"On it," Liam says, satisfied that Iola will be kept busy long enough to lend me a hand.

He stands and immediately almost falls over. The beating he has taken at the hands of Iola has clearly taken its toll. He doesn't give up or give in, though. He crouches down and then leaps fifteen feet into the air, drifting upward and landing in the projector room.

"Are you okay?" I ask.

Liam, more resilient than a desert cactus, brushes his imaginary troubles from his shoulder and forces a smile. "No skin off my human suit. Believe me, I've had worse. Now let's get on with it."

Liam scoops up what remains of the angel wings in his arms and hurls them through the hole in the wall. The sound they make when crashing to the floor below is deafening.

"Let's leap down there and drag them over to the barrel while the angel is tied up," Liam says, going over what remains of the plan out loud.

"Works for me."

It doesn't seem to work for Iola, however.

Having had enough of being restrained, the angel focuses her eyes on the tentacles. A burst of pale light pulses from her pupils like heavenly laser beams and cuts into the tentacles, shredding them to pieces and turning Boo-en's friend into nothing more than chunks of Pit sushi.

I only hope that the damage is not permanent. I know that hunting demons is kind of my thing, but whatever that creature was, it was still doing us a favor. I don't wish it any harm.

"Boo-en must be going now," I hear my paralysis demon shout from the depths of the portal.

As the lumps of tentacles fall to the floor, the malachite reforms into its natural shape and the portal to the underworld disappears.

Iola cracks her neck, savoring the sensation. She looks up at us. "I'll admit, you're far more capable than I thought you'd be. I am very seldom surprised. After all, I've been alive since the dawn of creation. But you have done just that. You have surprised me. I'm almost sorry that I have to kill you now."

In the distance, I can hear the unmistakable roar of The Fallen's motorcycles descending on the Marquee. The rest of the gang is here.

"This is our last chance," Liam says, his tone serious and stern.

I turn to look at my friend. I choose brutal honesty over motivational optimism. "You can't beat her."

Liam nods. "I don't have to beat her. I just have to get in a few good shots while you light those wings up."

Dread consumes me. "I can't lose you, Liam."

Liam lifts me up in his arms like a package ready for delivery and smiles. "I'm not one of your socks, Damon. You can't lose me!"

And with that, Liam drops down into the theater with me tucked under his arm. The wings are scattered all around our feet, and there are about twenty yards separating us and the holy oil fire—with one ticked-off angel standing in the way.

"Do you know what I dislike most about you being here?" Liam asks Iola as he props me up on my feet next to him.

Iola doesn't react. Instead, she just stares out at Liam and me, waiting for us to make the first move.

Liam decides to answer the question for her. "It's that you weren't content being The World Above's problem. Being a thorn in their side wasn't enough for you. You had to then go and become our problem, too."

Iola grins. "Well then, come on, demon swine. Show me what you've got!"

Without warning, Liam rockets through the air, traveling like a missile in Iola's direction.

"Burn the wings!" he shouts as he crashes into Iola, sending them both backward.

The pair battles as I work to drag the wings toward the fire. Unfortunately, there is too much debris blocking the aisle, and the wings are just too heavy for me to lift them over the broken seats and chunks of scattered drywall. No matter how hard I try, I can't do it. I can't save the day. I'm failing.

At my back, I hear the doors kicked open, ripped from their rusted hinges. I turn to find the other members of The Fallen arriving to the party. Their collective auras burn so bright that I stumble backward, slipping on angel feathers and falling hard on my rear.

"It's over," Iola says. I turn in her direction to see her standing over Liam. She has her foot pressed down into his chest, pinning him to the floor. "You've lost."

She runs her hand through the air, and in it appears her lance of pure light. She's going to smite Liam. She's going to murder my best friend.

I try to shout, but I can't. Fear has stolen my voice. It feels like I'm living in a nightmare that I can't wake up from.

Liam looks over to me, and I catch the slightest hint of a smile.

What is he up to?

He opens his hand conspicuously. In it, he is clutching the piece of malachite.

The trickster is readying himself to perform a trick.

"If you can't bring the wings to the fire, bring the fire to the wings," he says as Iola raises the pointy end of the lance over his chest.

I look around the theater. The old wooden seats. The highly flammable curtains that decorate the walls. The ancient studs that frame the building, which predate most fire safety regulations.

"This place is a tinder box," I mumble to myself.

"Salem is ours!" Iola declares as she brings the lance down on Liam.

Except by the time the point reaches Liam's chest, he isn't there. Instead, the lance jabs into the theater floor.

Once again, the malachite has turned into a portal, and this time, it has consumed Liam before he could be impaled.

"What?" a confused Iola wonders out loud.

I leap to my feet and run down the aisle. I can hear the other members of The Fallen chasing me, but they're too far away to reach me in time.

I make it to the steel barrel and turn to face Iola.

"Salem isn't yours," I say. "And it never was."

I hear the angels scream out as I kick the barrel over, releasing the blue flames from their steel prison.

12

The fire spits out from the barrel, sprinkling embers over the front row of wooden seats. Some of the freed flames quickly lose their fury and are choked out, but those that land on the upholstery take root.

The mushrooming flares become enraged and spread, building in both size and warmth. The flames crackle and spread off in different directions, looking like an octopus stretching out its tentacles. The fiery dance would be mesmerizing to look at if only I was watching from a safe distance. As it is, I don't really care for it very much. I need to get out of here soon.

Iola gasps as she realizes the danger that she and her gang are now in.

"You, meddling human dog!" she hisses. "I should have smote you the first time you stuck your nose into my business!"

"Should have, would have, could have," I say snidely.

Iola turns away from me to face her fellow Fallen members. Unable to think for themselves, they remain dumbfounded and motionless, staring at the spreading flames and awaiting orders.

"Well, don't just stand there, you imbeciles! Take action! Collect the wings! Collect my wings!"

Iola's command is too late, however. While The Fallen are tripping over themselves, Liam emerges from the malachite portal and collects the wings. They turn around, helpless as they see him standing behind them, holding their fate in his hands.

"I make one heck of a *wingman*," he says with a smirk. "Just ask my BFF Damon."

I can't help but smile at Liam's well-timed reappearance. If there's one thing you can always count on in life, it's that a trickster demon will never pass up an opportunity to fool a fool.

"Now just hold it right there," Iola says,

her outward anger subsiding. The tone of her voice turns friendly. She pleads with Liam. She knows that her life is in his hands. "We can give you whatever you want. This can all be water under the bridge. Fame? Fortune? Power? Name it! Whatever it is, if you pray for it, we can provide."

The flames continue to spread, jumping across rows of seats and moving up the wall with ease. The air becomes thick with smoke, and I'm forced to pull the collar of my shirt over my mouth and nose. It's the worst possible ventilation mask I could wear, but it's also all I have.

It's as if time has stopped. Everything slows down to a standstill.

Iola's negotiating tactics were directed at Liam, but I find myself considering her offer. Only, I'm not interested in anything she mentioned specifically—fame, fortune, or power. None of that is really my style. I'm only interested in one thing.

I want my mother back.

"Can you bring people back from the dead?"

I ask, surprising even myself as the words escape my mouth.

Liam's face scrunches up in genuine confusion. "Damon? What are you doing? Don't fall for her tricks!"

I hold my hand up to Liam, gesturing for him to wait before he does anything with the wings he's holding.

I turn to Iola, staring into her bright eyes. Her pupils spark with light, and I worry that she's going to laser beam me.

"Well, can you? People who have passed on—can you bring them back?"

The familiar grin returns to Iola's face. "Pray for it, and we can make anything happen."

"I pray for it every night, but it hasn't happened yet," I say, doubtful of what the rogue angel is promising.

The flames grow higher into the air, spreading to the ceiling. If Liam and I don't leave this theater soon, we may never get out alive.

"That was before you had friends in high places," Iola tells me. "We could end this whole ordeal right now with both of us happy—The

Fallen going on our way, and you having your loved one back."

Liam interjects himself into the negotiations. "Damon, you can't be considering this! She is so untrustworthy that The World Above tossed her out! Do you have any idea how difficult that is to pull off?"

Iola's head whips to the right so that she can face Liam. "Tell your friend that I can't do it then, demon swine. Go ahead . . . tell him that I'm lying."

Liam appears conflicted as the fire inches closer to him. "I won't lie to you, Damon. I won't. But just because she can do it doesn't mean it should be done. There are no guarantees that your mother will come back as the mother you knew her to be."

I stare down at my feet, watching a small trail of flames expand across my vision. I'm lightheaded, but I'm not sure if it's from inhaling the smoke or from the possibilities that have been laid out before me. The possibility of having my mom returned to me.

"What's it going to be?" Iola asks. "Do we

have a deal? Our wings for your mother?"

I take a deep breath and press my hands together. I close my eyes and lower my head.

And then I begin to pray.

13

Silence falls over the theater. The only sound that can be heard is the crackling of the thickening fire. Everyone—angels and demon—holds their breath as I pray.

"I love you, Mom," I whisper.

Iola's smile quickly fades. "Do not get any ideas, boy. Keep your prayer focused."

I continue to pray, though what I pray for is not to the angel's liking.

"Get my name out of your prayer!" Iola hisses.

I take a deep breath, hold it for five seconds, and then exhale. I finish my prayer with a wish for resolution.

"How dare you?" Iola spits with venomous hatred. Her fury returns with a vengeance.

Liam calls out to me from over the flames. "What did you do?"

I raise my head and open my eyes. It's difficult to see everyone through the smoke that hangs over the theater. I spot Liam, but he's more of a shape than the familiar face I've come to appreciate over our years of friendship.

"I prayed," I tell him. "I prayed that the fire would consume their wings and take the angels away from here!"

"Go, Damon!" Liam shouts as he hurls the angel wings into the air, throwing them toward the heart of the fire.

"I will not answer that prayer!" Iola screams.

The leader of The Fallen leaps with supernatural agility. She soars over the flames and plucks two wings from the air—like an eagle snatching its prey from the sky in its talons. She lets the other wings continue on their downward trajectory, causing her fellow gang members to count down the seconds until their extinction.

"No, Iola!" one of the fallen angels proclaims in a fearful cry. "You must save us all!"

Iola lands in the projector room as the

remaining angel wings plunge into the fire.

"I *must* do no such thing," Iola responds, clutching her wings tightly.

The feathers that make up the angels' wings erupt in flames as if they've been doused in gasoline. The flash of burning light illuminates the entire room. It looks like their very auras are burning alongside the wings. The smell of caramelized citrus attacks my senses, overpowering the smoke and causing my eyes to water.

Is angel smoke toxic?

I look over at the members of The Fallen and I'm reminded of the many victims of Mount Vesuvius. The infamous volcano erupted in 79 CE, covering the ancient Roman city of Pompeii in up to twenty feet of ash and pumice, a porous rock that originates from volcanoes. Those who couldn't escape the eruption were turned into calcified ash statues, preserving their final moments of life for future generations to marvel over like macabre artifacts.

I know all of this because Boo-en recently

spent a night reading a book to me about the most devastating volcanic eruptions of all time.

For The Fallen, however, their final moments will not be preserved for all time.

As their wings burn up and turn to cinders, so, too, do the angels. Their bodies become mounds of lifeless soot that are blown away in an unnatural gust of wind that seems to travel down from above. Their screams of agony remain present, however, holding my attention even as the heat from the fire begins to melt the rubber soles of my sneakers.

"She's gone," I hear Liam say from the other side of the fire.

I look up toward the hole in the projector room wall. It's empty. Iola and her wings are nowhere to be seen.

"We have to reach her before she gets away," Liam continues to say, running to the open doorway. He looks out into the lobby. "There's too much smoke. I can't see where she went."

I cough as that same smoke assaults my lungs. I nod and sidestep the fire, discovering that my path out of the room was only seconds away from being devoured by the flames. This is my last chance to escape the inferno.

"Hopefully, she didn't get too far," Liam says as he helps me over the collapsed doors. Together, we head out into the lobby, hopeful that my prayers will be answered and that Iola will finally be dealt with.

14

Smoke has begun to infiltrate the lobby, making it difficult to see. Liam and I duck down below the dark gray plume and scan the large room for any signs of Iola. A single white feather sits on the floor about five yards away, not far from the doors leading out of the Marquee.

"That way," I tell Liam, pointing over at Iola's fallen plumage.

Still crouched, we creep toward the evidence until daylight becomes visible through the smoke. The closer we get to the feather, the more we realize just how close to the front doors we are. And there she is, Iola, standing at the doors and looking shocked to discover that the Salem Library's Book Bus has been driven up the stairs and is now completely blocking the exit. Madelyn is seated behind the steering wheel, waving at us. She seems to be thoroughly enjoying herself.

Arson. Grand theft auto. Angel murder. We've really stepped in it this time. I'm not sure how we can get out of this situation without finding ourselves in some serious trouble. Not to mention that my dad is totally going to find out what I've been doing in my spare time. I guess I better get used to spending most of my free time in my bedroom. At least I have Mom's records to listen to.

Iola readies herself to power through the doors, but Liam drives his shoulder into her, knocking her away instead.

"Looks like your wings have been clipped," Liam tells Iola.

Like a cornered dog, Iola turns toward us and lashes out. She swats at me, connecting at my shoulder with a sledgehammer-like strike. The force sends me careening into the wall. Searing pain travels down my side, and I crash down to the floor in a heap.

The benefit of being knocked to the floor is that I'm now below the smoke line and can breathe much easier down here. Of course, I'm so badly injured that just breathing is proving to be a painful necessity, so I guess the bad kind of outweighs the good.

While I struggle to catch my breath, Liam is trying to muscle Iola's angel wings away from her. Unfortunately, while Liam is strong, his strength pales in comparison to an angel's. Iola is able to overpower him and knocks him backward into the blockaded doors, shattering the glass. She waves her hand in the air, once again summoning her lance of light. Without showboating this time, Iola presses the tip of the lance into Liam's neck, piercing his phony human flesh.

"Goodbye, demon swine," she says, drawing back the lance so that she can power it through my friend.

I can only watch helplessly from the floor as Iola drives her lance forward. As much as I want to close my eyes and make this nightmare go away, I keep them open out of respect for Liam. I want his final memory to be one of a friendly face.

Only, the lance stops just before reaching Liam's throat.

The lobby of the Marquee erupts in a penetrating light, which makes everything turn into jumbled shapes and squiggly lines. When it fades away, there is a white-haired man with a sharply sculpted jaw standing behind Iola. He has one hand on the lance as the other brushes soot off his light gray suit, which is a near-perfect color match for his hair.

Upon seeing the stranger, Iola's expression becomes one that I have yet to see her express—fear.

"You've been quite busy since leaving The World Above, Iola," the man says. "We've taken notice but have yet to intervene. Unfortunately for you, that is no longer an option."

"He's a demon!" Iola shouts, trying to pull her lance away from the man's grip. "I've seen you smite hundreds like him! Thousands even!"

The stranger tightens his grip on the lance. The weapon turns from pure light into something much more solid. He taps the handle with his finger, and it shatters into a million pieces of broken glass shards. Strangely, they make no sound when they hit the lobby floor.

"Nevertheless," the stranger continues, "your time on Earth has come to an end."

Panic overtakes Iola. "But why? Why intervene now?"

The man raises his hand and points an extended finger in my direction. "Because I heard the boy's prayer, and his prayer has been answered."

15

"You . . . you heard my prayer?" I ask, dragging myself to my feet despite the pain.

The man keeps his eyes on Iola as he responds to my question. "All of The World Above did. We were unable to intervene in Iola's actions here on Earth until one of His creations made such a request through the proper channels. There are rules we must follow—even in matters of our own."

"But you don't have to," Iola informs the stranger, pleading with him. "You could look the other way—we all could—and then I can just wander off. I'd bother no one ever again, especially these two." She gestures to Liam and me. "I'd lay forever low and keep my sinning to myself. Come on, you know me. We've served alongside each other for centuries. We fought demon hordes together. We watched the dawn of humankind side by side."

The stranger stands in silence. He appears to ponder the history that exists between them. Iola senses something in his hesitation that she can exploit and then pulls on those threads.

She smiles. "You know that you can have more fun down here with the human dogs, right? They're playthings. Pieces of clay to sculpt and mold as we see fit. And as it turns out, The Fallen just so happens to be a few riders short."

Her smile grows wide and eerie as she continues trying to convince him. "Think of the times we could have together down here! Those rules you just spoke about—they don't apply. Not here. Anything goes. So, what do you say? Why don't you join me down here on Earth? We'll ride together just as we fought together."

Without warning, the stranger's hand burns bright with light, and he thrusts it into Iola's abdomen. Her eyes go wide with surprise as the realization of her failure manifests in her punishment.

"Please," she begs, hoping for mercy. "I am one of you. We are the same. They are the enemy, not me."

The man twists his hand inside of her, turning it like a key in a lock.

Iola's human disguise falls away, her crumpled pink skin suit dropping to the floor like a discarded outfit. Beneath the flesh is nothing more than an orb of white light, which remains in the stranger's clutches. Inside the orb is the symbol I first witnessed within Iola's aura on the day she smote the demon dog.

Liam kneels down and picks up Iola's wings. He looks toward the theater. The flames, now incensed and seemingly unstoppable, fan out into the lobby. They are hungry to consume the entire building.

Liam takes one step toward the flames, only to be stopped by the stranger.

"I both understand and sympathize with your eagerness to confront the flames with Iola's wings, but burning them is unnecessary." He flicks his wrist, and Iola's wings disappear, leaving Liam empty-handed. "The fate that awaits Iola is far worse than anything your minds could possibly conceive. The punishment will be just."

He flicks his wrist a second time, and the orb of light that was once Iola also disappears.

"So, that's it?" Liam asks, annoyed. "The celestial cavalry arrives and makes the bad lady go away, and we're just supposed to go back out into the world and get on with our lives?"

The man slowly turns to face us. His expression hasn't changed since he arrived—not a single eyebrow raise or twitch of the nose.

"Do you require something else?" he asks.

I step forward, taking small, shallow breaths to keep from choking on the smoke.

"Is it true that angels can make any prayer come true?" I ask him, once again catching Liam off guard. "Iola told us it was possible."

"Damon, not this again," Liam moans.

I shush him, which I know he will hold against me later. It won't matter, though—none of it will matter—if the stranger can give me what I want.

The man slowly nods. "With me here, in

your presence, all prayers can be answered."

I acknowledge what the stranger has told me, and I press my hands together. I close my eyes and bow my head. And once again . . . I pray.

After a few moments of inner dialogue, I open my eyes and fix them on the stranger.

"You do know that if I answer this prayer, it will change everything," the man informs me.

"I do," I tell him.

"Damon?" Liam pleads, trying to talk me out of it. "As your friend, please don't do this."

I turn to look at Liam. "I need you to trust me," I say. "I'm not asking for what you think I'm asking for. I just want this mess cleaned up. I want everything to go back to normal like before the angels arrived."

Liam takes a deep breath and steps back. He's putting his trust in me.

"Very well," the man says. "Repairs will be made. Injuries will be mended. But you will remember nothing of this ordeal, nor of our existence."

And with that, a flash of light fills the lobby, temporarily blinding me. The light fades.

I look around at my surroundings, trying to make sense of where I am and how I got here. Am I dreaming? None of this looks familiar to me. Is this some kind of movie theater lobby? It kind of looks like the place my grandpa used to tell me about.

"Are we inside the Marquee?" I hear Liam ask. I turn to find him opening the door to what appears to be the theater, its interior perfectly preserved from its heyday. "Did you demon-nap me and bring me here as some kind of practical joke or something? If so, not cool, Damon!"

I shake my head. "I have no idea how we got into this place, but I know I'm going to be in tons of trouble if my dad finds out I've been here. He just told me to stay away from the Marquee. He didn't want us anywhere near it. Apparently, there's been some kind of motorcycle gang in town who has been using this spot as their hangout. He thinks they're dangerous."

Liam pokes around some more, inspecting the dusty relic of a building. "I think your dad has the wrong intel this time. It doesn't look like there's been anyone here for decades."

I shrug and then grab hold of Liam's shirt, pulling him toward the front doors. "Come on. Let's just get the heck out of here and figure out *how* we got here later."

I inhale, which prompts a cough to build in my throat and then escape my body. My lungs feel like I've been sitting by a campfire all day. I don't know what that's all about, but I'll just group it with the rest of today's unexplained occurrences.

Maybe Boo-en will be able to help me make sense of all of this. Could it be some kind of time displacement issue? Or maybe a trickster trick? (Not Liam, of course, but maybe some other trickster who is operating in Salem?)

"Do you smell citrus?" Liam asks as I pull him out through the front doors of the Marquee and then step out into the fresh air of the day.

I don't know what's going on, but right now, all I want to do is go home and listen to my mom's old records. Hearing her voice always makes me feel better.

She had the voice of an angel.

ABOUT THE AUTHOR

When not writing in his spiral notebooks, Jason M. Burns can be found outside getting his tattoo-covered arms dirty where he spends the warmer months hybridizing daylilies and tending to his koi pond. Type A even when typing, he has written and created a number of critically-acclaimed and commercially successful comic book series and graphic novels, including *Magical Pet Vet* and *Jericho: Season 3*, which appeared on the *New York Times* Best Sellers list. He has spearheaded book lines for *Sesame Street* and the DreamWorks Animation stable of titles and most recently served as Chief Creative Officer for Neymar Jr. Comics, the publishing company of international soccer star Neymar Jr. There his writing was translated across six languages and reached over forty million people worldwide. In addition to comic books, Burns also works in Hollywood where he has a number of television and film projects in development. He is also co-host of the popular podcast series *What About*, which he produces alongside actor Danny Nucci (*Titanic*, *The Fosters*).

Burns lives in Massachusetts with his wife, two children, and a trio of rescue dogs with unnecessarily silly names, Bark W. Grizwold, Maisy Gray, and Bad Bad Leroy Brown.